George E. Foster

One Line of the Farley Family

George E. Foster

One Line of the Farley Family

ISBN/EAN: 9783337312558

Printed in Europe, USA, Canada, Australia, Japan

Cover: Foto ©Raphael Reischuk / pixelio.de

More available books at **www.hansebooks.com**

CASTLE FALAISE, NORMANDY·

ONE LINE

OF THE

FARLEY FAMILY.

—

1. GEORGE, from England.
2. CALEB, b. 1645.
3. BENJAMIN, b. 1685.
4. BENJAMIN, b. 1708.
5. EBENEZER, b. 1747.
6. JESSE, b. 1781.
7. SOPHIA P., b. 1825.
8. GEORGE E. FOSTER, b. 1849.
9. JESSE W., b. 1880.

—

BY GEO. E. FOSTER.

—

WEST HILL PRESS,
ITHACA, NEW YORK.
1897.

"What more precious testimonial of your love of kindred and home can you leave than that which provides for the transmission of the history of your ancestors, yourself and family, to future generations." Hon. Marshall P. Wilder.

VIRTUTE DUCE COMITE FORTUNA

HERALDRY.

FARLEY OF WARWICKSHIRE.

CREST.

ANTELOPE'S HEAD ERASED PIERCED THROUGH THE NECK WITH A SHORT SPEAR. PPR.

ARMS.

PER PALE SABLE AND OR.

MOTTO.

VIRTUTE DUCE COMITE FORTU-NA.

WHEN HONOR LEADS VICTORY ATTENDS.

Time hath intermingled and confused all, and we are come all to this present by successive variable descendants from high and low; or as Lee saith more plainly, the low are descended from the high, and contrariwise, the high from the low.

THE
FARLEY FAMILY.

Bristol, a place of great antiquity, an important maritime city in the West of England, upon the rivers Frame and Avon, partly in the countries of Gloucester and Somerset, was the early home of one Fabyan Farley. He married Jane Hungerford of Farleigh Castle, Somersetshire. They had seven children, and most of the Farleys now living in America can trace their pedigree to this marriage. The Farley name is one of the oldest in England. It can be traced back to the home of William the Conqueror,

Castle Falaise in Normandy, A. D. 100 ?
Duke Robert, before starting on his jour-
ney of pilgrimage to the Holy Land, left
his castle in the custody of William and
Walter, as Lords of Falaise, and upon
his death, Walter, being the eldest, became the Lord, and William became the
Conqueror, as is shown in English history. Walter had a son, William, who
went with his half brother to England.
as Williamus De Falaise, to whom was
given twenty-six lordships in county Dev-
on. In tracing the pedigree of the Farley
family, starting with De Falaise, eleven
different spellings of the name are found :
De Falaise, Ffar-lea, Ffarle, Farle, Fair-
ley, Farlea, Farly, Farlo, Farlegh, Far-
lee, Farley.

Fabyan Farley, who, as mentioned
above, married Jane Hungerford, was a

lescendant of this before mentioned Williamus De Falaise. After his marriage
he resided in Torothorpe County, York,
England, where he had two sons. His
first son, Thomas, was born in 1602. His
second son, George, was born in 1615.
'n the lives of these two sons of Fabyan
Farley the American Farleys have spec-
ial interest. Thomas emigrated to Vir-
ginia, with his wife and one servant,
Nicholas Shotter. They landed at Ar-
cher's Hook, a projection of land opposite
Jamestown, Va., 4 Feb. 1624, on the ship
Anne, the third ship after the May
Flower. They had a child, Anne, named
in honor of the ship that brought them
over. She was the first Farley born in
America. But the movements of Fabyan's
other son, George, are of the greatest
interest to those for whom this brochure

is written. He emigrated to America in
1640. He came to this country on the ship
Lion, and landed at Charleston or Roxbury. The cause of his coming to this
country may be found in the religious
persecution of those days growing out
of the differences between Protestant dis-
senters and the Church of England.
Soon after his arrival in this country he
moved to Woburn, Mass., where he married 9 April, 1641, Christian Births, a
Swede, who had come over in the same
ship. She was an orphan, her father having died at sea in the passage over. They
lived at Woburn until the year 1653, his
name being on the first list of county tax
assessed at Woburn, 8 September, 1645.
this being the first on record. In 1653
they moved to Shawshin, afterward
known as Billerica, Mass., where they

were among the first settlers of that ancient village.

On 19 Nov., 1656, he disposed of his house and lot of twenty acres at Woburn to Richard Snow. From Fisher's Genealogy we quote :

In 1660 George Ffarley is corporal in the Trayne Band. That year he was a committee to treat for half an acre in the town's behalf for a burial place. In 1677 he was appointed one of the five tithing men. Soon after his arrival at Billerica, in 1653, purchased the northwest lot of the Dudley farm, where he resided near the Jaquith place; his occupation being given as clothier or draper. Upon this place he had erected a commodious and substantial dwelling, which the town records note as being used for a garrison in the year 1676, during King Philip's war.

This house, with adjoining land of twenty acres, has since been in possession of his descendants. The old house, at the present time, is in a good state of preservation. Mr. Franklin Jaquith, a descendant of Ebenezer Farley, who is in possession of this property, says, in reference to the old Farley homestead :—

"There is recorded at Cambridge, Mass., an agreement whereby Caleb Farley, Jr., received the homestead and other property, in consideration of taking care of his aged grandfather, George Farley, and grandmother during their lifetime. April 6th, 1706, Caleb Farley, Jr., deeded it to his brother, Joseph Farley. June 9th, 1720, Benjamin Farley deeded the same as sold to him by his brother Joseph, to his brother, Ebenezer Farley. The date that Joseph conveyed it to Benjamin I could not ascertain. May 20th. 1728, Ebenezer Farley, 'for in consideration of the love and affection which I have and do have unto my daughter, Hannah Farley, wife of Abraham Jaquith Jr., of Woburn.' deeded the same to Abraham Jaquith, Jr. After which its owners were: Joseph Sr., Joseph Jr., and his widow, Franklin Sr., and at present time the house is owned by myself. On the place is pointed out where once was an Indian burying ground. Tradition has also located a spot where stood a wigwam. Many relics were found here in my father's early days. Here also was the first birth in Billerica—'Samuel Farley, born 1654, March ye last week.'"

Oct. 9th, 1659, George Farley was one of the church building committee.

Aug. 7th, 1660, according to a record:

"The towne doe give leave that Ralph Hill, Sen'r, George Farley, Willm. French, Ralph Hill, jun'r, and John Parker and such other persons as make use of their horses to Ride to ye meetings, shall have liberty to make sum housing or housings to sett up for horses from time to time, without molestatione, and to sett up ye saide housing below the Hill between the meeting-house and Golden More's barn, or in sum other place convenient for them."

During the years 1661, 1662, 1666, 1669 and 1688, George Farley was a select man of Billerica.

In those days Puritans were often arrested for heresy, and according to the records, on June 18th, 1672, George Farley, Thomas Foster and William Hamlet were before the Middlesex County Court, being presented for breach of the ecclesiastical laws. They all confessed the presentment, were admonished and ordered to pay costs. 4s. 6d., for worshiping the God of their fathers in the way which the judges called heresy.

Religiously George (1) was a Baptist.

He was a member of the First Baptist church in Boston. Fisher says of him :—
"He was a man of influence in the early history of collonial affairs at Billerica. He died at Billerica 27 Dec., 1693, and Christian his widow died 27 March, 1702.

In 1675. on account of the troubles with the Indians under King Philip, sachem of the Wamponoags, the court of the colony advised the establishment of twelve garrisons, located in twelve different places, for the protection of the people. One of those was at George Farley's house. George and his son took active part in the Indian war, Timothy, his son, being killed by the Indians, 2 Aug., 1675. He was the first to be killed in the contest. The fight was near the head of Wickaboag Pond. There is a record, showing that George Farley was given credit for military service in Capt. Thomas Wheeler's company to the amount of £14.

This contest is described by Drake as follows :—

"Soon after the war began, Massachusetts, fearing the Nipmuks might join with Philip, sent messengers to treat with them. The young Indians were found 'surly,' but the old men were for a renewal of friendship ; but the person or persons sent upon this business did not acquit themselves in a manner that gave satisfaction ; and Philip, being now in the

country of the Nipmuks, it was conclu-
ded by the authorities of Massachusetts to
make a further test of their intentions.
Accordingly, on the 28 July, Captains
Hutchinson and Wheeler, with a company of 20 mounted men, and 3 Christian
Indians as pilots and interpreters, viz.
Memecho, Joseph and Sampson, went
with some of the inhabitants of Brookfield,
agreeably to appointment, to meet the
Nipmuk sachems. It had been agreed by
these sachems to meet the English in a
treaty at a certain tree at Quabaog on the
2 August, on a plain 3 miles from Brookfield village. Having arrived here according to agreement, the English found
no Indians to treat with. It was now a
question with all but the Brookfield men,
whether or not they should proceed to a
certain place where they believed the In-

dians to be ; at length the confidence of the Brookfield people in the pacific disposition of the Indians, prevailed, and they marched on. The way was so bad that they could march only in single file as they approached the place where they expected to find the Indians, and when they came near Wikabaug Pond, between a swamp on the left and a very abrupt and high hill on the right, snddenly 2 or 300 Indians rose up, encompassed, and fired upon them. Eight were killed outright, and three fell mortally wounded. Captains Hutchinson and Wheeler were both mortally wounded. The latter's son, although his arm was broken by a bullet seeing his father's peril, dismounted from his horse, and succeeded in mounting his father upon it.. A retreat now began, and by cutting their way through the Indians, the small remnant of English got back to Brookfield.

THE TRIBE OF GEORGE AND CHRISTIAN.

—o—

The Children of George and Christian Births Farley were seven in number; the first five were born in Woburn, the rest in Billerica. They were as follows:

Children born at Woburn:
    i. James, b. Nov. 23d. 1643:
          d. Dec 10th, 1643. ·
2.   ii. Caleb, b. April 1st, 1645:
          d. March, 16th, 1645.
    iii. Mary, b. Feb. 27th, 1647;
          m. John Sanders.
    iv. Timothy, b.
    killed. by Indians, Aug 2nd, 1675.
    v. Elizabeth, b.

Children born at Billerica, Mass:
    vi. Samuel, b. last week in March, 1654; the first child born at Billerica.
    vii. Mehetabell, b. last week in May, 1656;   d. Feb. 1st, 1672.

THE TRIBE OF CALEB [2].
LYDIA AND REBECCA.

—o—

Caleb Farley, son of George and Christian Births Farley, born, April 1st, 1645, at Woburn, Mass; died March 16, 1712, at Billerica; married, first, July 5th, 1666, Rebecca, daughter of Ralph Hill; she died March 25th, 1669; he married, on Nov, 2nd, 1669, Lydia, daughter of Golden More. She died Nov. 19th, 1715. After 1671, he resided in Woburn until May, 1679, when he exchanged homesteads with William Himlet and returned to Billerica. Later he went to Roxbury, but came back to reside with Golden More.

Issue by wife Rebecca.

    i. Caleb, b. June, 28th, 1667.

    ii. Rebecca, b. March 10, 1669;
             m. Thomas Frost.

Issue by wife Lydia:

    iii. Lydia, b. Sept. 27th, 1670;
             m. Zachary Shed.

    iv. Hannah, b. Oct. 18th, 1671.

    v. Ebenezer, b. April, 3d, 1674;
    m. Jan. 6th, 1703 to Elizabeth Shed.

    vi. George, b. July 30th, 1677.

    vii. Timothy, b. July 29th, 1680.

    viii. Joseph, b. April 6th, 1683; m.,
    May 8th, 1712, to Abagail Cook,

3   ix. BENJAMIN, b. Feb. 8th, 1685-6;
    m., Oct. 29th. 1707, to Ann Dunton.

    x. Enoch, b. Dec. 21st. 1688.

THE TRIBE OF BENJAMIN[3]
AND ANN DUNTON.

—o—

Benjamin Farley, son of Caleb and Lydia Moore Farley, b. at Billerica, on Feb. 8th, 1685, m. Anna Dunton of Roxbury, Oct. 29th, 1707, and had

4   i. BENJAMIN, b. Aug. 28th, 1708.

     ii. Sarah, b. Feb. 8th, 1709.

     iii. Anna, b. Nov. 15th, 1711.

     iv. Samuel, b.   1718; m. 9th, Oct.,1744, Hannah Brown.

All of the above children were born in Billerica.

BENJAMIN FARLEY [4]

Lt. Benjamin Farley, Jr. 4,—Benjamin
3. Caleb 2. George 1,—was born in Bedford, Mass., August 28th, 1708. He married Joanna Page, daughter of Christopher Page, who was son of Christopher 1.
They moved from Bedford to West Dunstable. He was one of the petitioners for
the town charter, the address being "To
his Excellency, Jona Belcher, Esq.,
Captain General and Governor in chief,
etc : the Hon. the Council and House of
Representatives in General Court Assem-
bled, at Boston, Nov. the 29th, 1736."

"The Petition of the subscribers, Inhabitants and Proprietors of the Towns of
Dunstable and Groton Humbly sheweth,
etc." See pages 34 and 35 Hollis history.

He was the first Inn keeper in West Dunstable. He lived first about one-fourth of a mile south of Hollis meeting house, where T. G. Worcester so long resided.

The first parish meeting under the parish charter was held at the inn of Lieut. Benjamin Farley, Jan. 22, 1739-40. Mr. Farley's inn was the place where the parish meetings were commonly held until the first meeting house was built.

At the first parish meeting he was elected one of the assessors, and was one of the committee "to procure preachin till the first of April following." He was one of the twenty-nine to pay the first parish tax of £16, 2s, 2d.

At the first town election in Hollis, as provided by the charter, Benjamin Farley was elected one of the Selectmen. He was parish assessor in 1740 and 1741.

In 1741, he was appointed a committee with others, " to take some proper measures to bring forward the settling of Larned and Other Dox Minister in this P arish as soon as conveniency will allow."

In 1745, he was one of the building committee of the second meeting house, and one of the authorized parties to raise funds for the same.

In 1744, he was one of the petitioners, second on the list, for military relief for the town. See pages 96 and 97 Hollis history.

THE TRIBE OF BENJAMIN FARLEY [4] and JOANNA PAGE.

Benjamin Farley (4) b. 28 Aug., 1708, m.——Joanna Page, who was daughter of Christopher Page, son of Nathaniel (1). She was born 10 Aug., 1717: her mother's name was Joanna——

The following were the children of Lt. Benjamin Farley and his wife, Joanna:—

   i.   Joanna, b. 21 April, 1733; m 2 June, 1754, Samuel Burge.

   ii. Rebecca, b. 29 April, 1735.

  iii. Benjamin, b. 21 June, 1737; m. 18 June, 1780, Lucy Fletcher of Dunstable.

  iv. Molly, b. 25 Nov. 1739; m. 9 Dec. 1779, John Shattuck.

   v. Betty, b. 23 June, 1742; m. 24 Nov., 1768, Benj. Asten.

  vi. Lucy, b. 13 Feb. 1744 m. 24 Nov., 1768, Abel Shipley.

5   vii. EBENEZER, b. 19th Sept., 1747, m. 6th Nov., 1776. Betty Wheeler.

  viii. Hannah, b. 8th Feb., 1750, d.

   ix. Christopher, b. 1st April, 1751; m. 30th Dec., 1773, Ruth Jewett, b. 10th May, 1753; d. 3d June, 1843.

    x. Stephen, b. 28th Jan. 1754; m. 28th Jan., 1779, Mary Shattuck; d. 13th Jan, 1837.

   xi. Hannah,' b. 31st Jan., 1757; m. 4th Dec., 1777, John Ball of Temple.

  xii. Sarah, b 28th Sept., 1761; m. Wm. Pool.

Speaking of his rank as Lieutenant, Hollis history says, on page 95 :—

"As we find in the Hollis records, shortly after the appointment of Captain

Powers, the title of Lieutenant prefixed to the name of Benjamin Farley,. of Ensign to that of Jerahmael Cumings, and of Sergeant to the name of James Stewart, there can be but little doubt that those persons held the offices indicated, in the first militia company of West Dunstable.

Three of his sons, Ebenezer, Christopher and Stephen, were in the Revolutionary war.

Benjamin (5) died Dec. 23, 1787, aged 79 years. Joanna died Aug. 20, 1797, aged 80. She was eminent for industry, piety and usefulness, and at the time of her death was the natural parent of 200 offspring—so the grave-stone says.

TRIBE OF EBENEZER FARLEY.
[5] and BETTY WHEELER.

Ebenezer (5). b. 19 Sept. 1747; m. Betty Wheeler, 6 Nov., 1766. They had children as follows ;—

i. Benjamin, (6) b. 1. Feb., 1767, m. Anna Merrill.

ii. Lucy, b, 3 Sept., 1768; m. 17 Jan., 1789, James Jewett.

iii. Joanna, b. 22 March, 1770; m. 15 Nov., 1792, Abijah Shedd.

iv. Betty, b. 18 March, 1772.

v. Ebenezer, b. 4 March, 1774; m. 12 Sept 1796, Abagail Farmer ;

vi. Hannah, b. 1 Dec., 1775; m. 25 Aug., 1791, Solomon Wheeler.

vii   John, b. 13 Dec., 1777.

viii.   Daniel, b. 28 Oct., 1779: went to Michigan.

6. ix.   JESSE. b. 26 June, 1781: m. Oct. 1. 1803, Mary Phelps, daughter of Nathan, 6; John 5; john 4; Sam- 3; Edward 2; Henry 1 of Salem.

x.   Sarah, b. 23 April. 1783; m. Minott Wheeler.

xi.   Rebecca, b. 15 Dec. 1784. m.—Gibbs.

xii.   Susannah, b. 3 Feb. 1787; m. 1 Jan, 1806, Wm. Fletcher Phelps.

xiii.   James, b. 21 May, 1791; m. Jane Wright.

Ebenezer 6 died 28 Jan., 1827, in his 80th year. He had a good record as a revolutionary soldier; he was at Lexington, and served two months in N. Y. in 1776..

Jesse Farley (6), the ninth child of Ebenezer (5) and Betty Wheeler, was born 26 June, 1781. Married 17 October, 1803, Mary Phelps of Hollis, who was daughter of Nathan Phelps, who married Mary Fletcher, and whose father was John Phelps of Andover, who married Deborah Lovejoy.

The children of Jesse Farley (7) and his wife Mary Phelps, are as follows :—

i. Mary, b. 1 July, 1804.

ii. Jefferson, b. 10 Jan. 1807.

iii. Leonard, b. 17 March, 1809.

iv. Mark, b. 21 March, 1811.

v. John b. 10 May, 1813.

vi ⎱ twins ⎰ Albert ⎱ b. 28 March '15.
vii ⎰   ⎱ Alfred ⎰

viii. Susan, b. 13 March, 1817.

ix. ⎱ twins ⎰ Jefferson. ⎱ b.19 Aug '19.
x. ⎰   ⎱ Harriett. ⎰

xi. Sophia b. 25 May, 1825.

His youngest child was one and a half years old at the time of his death. Jesse Farley lived, from the time of his marriage, on the homestead farm, caring for his aged father and mother during their declining years. He was of a genial, happy disposition, and had excellent standing in the community. He was a devout Christian, and a member of the Congregational church. He was careful to have his children baptized in infancy, but for some reason the baptism of the last was delayed. The family of boys who grew up were honest, well-to-do farmers. All the girls were members of the church. Four of the boys were church members, another died in infancy, and two others were Universalists, owing to influences outside the family. His wife was also a devout Christian, but the anxiety caused by the care of her fatherless children,—a victim of overwork—her health failed, her mind became affected, and one night while her children slept, by her own hand, she entered into another life.

DESCENDANTS OF MARY [7].

Mary, first child of Jesse Farley and Mary Phelps; b. 13 July, 1804; d. 29 Jan. 1870; m.——John Hardy of Hollis. They had five children :—

i.   Mary, d. June 1842, aged 19 yrs.

ii. John Jackson, d. Nov., 1826, age. 14 mos.

iii. Sarah A., b. 10 Oct, 1827; d. 23 Jan, 1877.

iv   Caroline, d, 6 Sept. 1833, aged 3 yrs, 11 mos.

v.   Susan, d. 13 March, 1836; age 11 months.

Sarah A. Hardy(8) b. 10 Oct., 1827; d. 23 Jan., 1877; m. 2 April, 1850, William Winslow Greenwood, who was born 21 June, 1825. They had first, Minott Winslow Greenwood(9), b. 30 July, 1854, who m. 23 June, 1878, Ida Achacy Wallace, b. 9 August, 1857. They had Clara Burns, b. 5 Dec., 1879, and Elsie May, b. 21 Oct, 1886. Sarah A. and William W. Greenwood had second, Mary Ellen(9), b. 2 Oct. 1861; m. John Hamblin of Augusta, Me., 18 June, 1888; d. 8 Sept., 1895, leaving Marion Louise(10), b. 19 April, 1889; Edith, b. 21 Aug., 1892.

ii. JEFFERSON.

Jefferson, b. 10 January, 1807, d. 12 Feb., 1815.

His life was short, but he left in his name the imprint of the political faith of Jesse Farley and his sons. They were, and the daughters, too. Jeffersonian Democrats. The first Jefferson, by Jesse, was born when Jeffersonian politics were at high heat—even the very year when that President Jefferson issued his famous proclamation requiring all armed vessels bearing commissions under the Government of Great Britain within the harbors of the United States, to immediately and without any delay depart from the same, and interdicting the entrance of all the said harbors and waters to the said armed vessels and to all others, bearing commissions under the authority of the British Government.

DESCENDANTS OF LEONARD [7].

Leonard (7), b. 19 March, 1809; d. 16 Nov. 1891; m. Sally Mooar, 2 September, 1830, who was born on eight July, 1810, daughter of Jacob Mooar and Dorcas Hood. She died 28 February, 1880. They had issue as follows :—

i. Leonard Jason, (8) b. 9 Nov., 1833; m. 3 October, 1860, Anna Carlton, who d. 18 Aug., 1895. They had

(1) Frank L., b. 17 Jan., 1865.

(2) Charles J., b. 23 Jan. 1867. who m. 2 Sept. 1890, Ella Pierce, and had 1 January, 1896,

(a) Earl Dexter [10].

ii.   Henrietta Sophia, b. 26 June,
      1836; d. 12 Sept. 1869; m. Rich-
      mond Parker, 5 Dec,, 1861, and
      had—

> (1) Nelly H., b. 17   Sept.
>   1863. m. 22 Dec., 1885.
>   Frank P. Dow, who d.
>   childless, 29 Sep., 1895.

> (2) Fred. b. 18 Jan., 1865.
>   Went to California.

iii, Albert J., b. 15 Feb. 1844; m. 8
      Dec. 1870, Etta F. Wheeler; had
      Kate F., b. 26 Sept., 1872; she m.
      25 Nov., 1896, Herbert Spaulding,
      son of Albert Spaulding.

iv.   E. B. Hammond b. 27 June, 1846.
      d. 11 Oct. 1862.

v.   Charles Monroe, b. 17 June, 1850.
      d. 21 Sept., 1852.

vi.   Frank Pierce. b. 26 March, 1853,
      d. 7 April, 1855.

DESCENDANTS OF MARK FAR-LEY[7] AND MARY CROSBY.

Mark(7). b. 21 Jan., 1811 ; d. 22 June, 1872 ; m. 25 Aug., 1834, at South Merrimack, N. H. Mary Swan Crosby, b. 1 March, 1818 ; d. 6 May, 1885. They had :—

i.   Mary Ann(8), b. Hamilton, Ohio, 21 June, 1835 ; d. 9 Aug., 1835.

ii. Susan Elizabeth(8), b. in Hamilton Ohio, 27 July, 1836 ; m. at Milford N. H., 11 Nov., 1862, Frank I. Abbott, and had :—

   (1) Fred F.(9) b. 16 Aug., 1865 ; m. 14 Jan., 1891, Olive S. Perry of Charlestown, Mass., and had

Marion Perry (10), b. 19 July. 1893: d. 22 july, 1893.

(2) Estella Farley Abbott, b. 7 April, 1868 ; m. 13 June 1889, Charles Sumner Emerson, and had :—

(a) Dean Abbott(10), b. 26 April, 1892.

(b) Sumner Brooks, b. 3 Jan., 1895.

iii. Mary Crosby, b. 31 May, 1838 ; d. 16 Sept., 1841.

iv. William Albert, b. 30 June, 1842 ; died of accidental poisoning at Ellendale, Dakota Territory, 30 June, 1887 ; m. Anna E. Mellen, at Rome, Mich., 3 April, 1866, and had :—

(1) Arthur M. b. 27 Feb. '67

(2) Nina M., b. 3 Jan., 1869

(3) Allison A. b. 24 Mar. '71

(4) Carl C. b 18 March, 1873

v Harriett Alice, b. 6 Dec., 1845 ; m. at Imlay City, Mich., 25 March. 1868, Seymour H. Sleeper : d. 6 Nov., 1892. No issue

vi. Catherine Kellogg Farley, b. 10 March, 1849 ; m. 13 Nov., 1875, at Imlay City, Edward E. Palmer. No issue.

vii. Ella Sophia, b. 24 April, 185? ; d. 8 Aug., 1875 ; m. 3 Sept., 1872, at Almont, Mich., Henry Sanford. Left Louis Sanford, b. 7 April, 1874, who in 1897 lived in Jackson Mich.

viii. Charles Kellogg(8), b. 31 July,

1854 ; m. at Imlay City, 1 Jan., 1880, Henrietta Mair, and had :—

(1) Mark Mair, b. 18 Nov. '80

(2) Fred Abbott b. 15 May '84

(3) Jean Hamilton, b. 23 Feb. 1886.

(4) James Ronald b. 4 Oct.'89

(5) Albert Walter, b.15 Sept. 1891.

(6) Howard Lee. b. 17 Aug., 1895.

JOHN FARLEY [7].

John Farley (7), b. May 10, 1813, m. Hannah Blood, 7th June, 1837, who died 16th September, 1890. Had children as follows :—

i. Hannah Sophia, b. 6 June, 1839, d. 2 January, 1859.

ii. Caroline, b. 16 April, 1843, d. 4 January, 1860.

iii Susan, b. 16 August, 1845, d. 16 August, 1860.

These children all died of consumption. John Farley was Selectman in 1842 and 1843, and was member of the House of Representatives in 1853 and 1854.

Leonard (7) also was member of the Board of Selectmen for the town of Hollis, in the years 1835, 1836 and 1839. He represented the town in the legislature in 1840, 1841 and 1842.

ALBERT AND ALFRED [7].

Albert and Alfred (7) (twins), b. 28 March, 1815. Albert (no date) married widow Sarah Fulsom. Died childless, 13 January, 1840. Alfred married 31 Aug., 1837, Lydia Farley, who d. 25 Nov., 1863. They had Roanna, b. 20 April, 1839; m. 1 July, 1859, Asa B. Eaton, and had Alfred Farley and Roanna Lillie, twins, b. 4 November 1865. Alfred Farley(7) m. 2nd, 19 Oct., 1865, Mary W. Eastman of Amherst.

DESCENDANTS OF SUSAN [7].

Susan (7) b. 13 March, 1817; d. 2 Dec., 1890; m. 29 Jan., 1845, Rufus N. Wallingford of Milford, who was murdered 10 Aug., 1875. He was a descendant of Nicholas Wallington, who came over from England in the ship Confidence in 1638, and settled in Newbury, Mass. He married and had several children. Early in 1670's he made a voyage to the coast of Barbary and never returned. At his death his family adopted the name of Wallingford. Susan had :—

   i. Eliza Ann, b. 16 June, 1846; d. 29, Aug., 1849.

ii. Charles Rufus, b. 4 July, 1849, m.
1st, 10 Oct., 1874, Ida Fletcher,
and had :—

(1) Peletiah Fletcher, b. 12
Oct., 1875.

(2) Richard Needham, b. 30
Jan., 1877.

Charles Rufus married, 2nd, Jan.,
1897, Sophronia L. Roberts, who
was born in Masamiscontis, Me.,
6 Aug. 1862.

iii. Emma Frances (8), b. 10 May,
1853; m. 27 Nov., 1873, Charles
R. Howard. Had no children.

iv. Horace Arthur (8), b. 30 March,
1863; m. 12 Oct. 1887, Josephine
Porter Caffrey, who was born at
Waterville, Me., 7 Dec., 1865.
They had :—

(1) Miriam C., b. 30 March '90

(2) Howard, b. 26 Jan., 1892.

In 1897, Charles resided in Montague Maine; Emma Frances at Birmingham, Conn, and Arthur in Dorchester.

JEFFERSON AND HARRIETT [7]

Jefferson and Harriett(7), twins, b. 19 Aug., 1819. Jefferson m. 15 Sept., 1842, Charlotte M. Farley. No issue. Jefferson Farley was always a sterling Democrat, and knew no compromise in the principles of Democracy. He was one of the selectmen of the town in 1861 and 1862. He will ever be remembered as one of the substantial, well-to-do citizens of Hollis. Harriett d. 18 Dec., 1884; m. 29 Jan., 1845, Nathaniel G. Furnald, who was born 2 Feb. 1818; d. 28 Nov., 1873 He was a substantial contractor and builder at Lowell Mass. They had :—

i. Frank B., b. 25 Dec., 1845; m. 3
    Sept., 1867, Lucy M. Cambridge,
    and had :—

        (1) Fred Wright, b. 17 Dec.,
            1868; m. Grace Louise
            Horsfall, 14 June. 1893,
            who had :—

                (a) Sara Louise,
                    b. 2 Dec., '95.
        (2) Nellie, b. 1 Dec., 1874.

ii. Charlotte M. Furnald(8), b. 3 Feb.,
    1851. After her parents death she
    resided with Jefferson Farley at
    Hollis, N. H.

Sophia P. b. 25 May, 1825 ; m. 15 Feb. 1848, to John E. Foster of Milford, and had :—

i. George Everett, b. 27 Aug., 1849 ; m. 14 July, 1874, Mary L Burritt, daughter of Rev. Chas. D. Burritt, of Ithaca, N. Y., and had :—

(1) Jesse Webster(9), b. 11 Feb. '80. George (8) was a journalist in Milford, N. H., thirteen years. Moved to Ithaca, N. Y., in 1887. Speaking of his journalistic work in New Hampshire, Governor G. A. Ramsdell wrote in Hillsborough County History :—

SOPHIA PHELPS FOSTER.

"The Milford 'Enterprise" is skill-
fully edited by George E. Foster,
Esq., and is highly valued by the
citizens of this town, as it is by those
living elsewhere who have an interest in all that concerns her people.
The paper was started by Mr. Foster
in 1873, and has always been a help-
ful moral force in the community,
and a source of much pleasure to its
readers." See also Foster Family,
page 28.

ii. Flora Sophia(8), b. 18 April, 1866;
m. George N. Woodward, 27 Oct
1886.

It should be mentioned here, that the
name, Sophia, is a substitute for Zeru-
iah. Sophia 7 through life was a constant
student of the Scriptures ; her life was that
of a consistent Christian ; and so far as
seems possible in the range of human pos-
sibilities she followed to the very letter the
teachings of the Bible that she daily read.

A FARLEY PATRIARCH.

Many of the descendants of George (1) attained an age greater than the allotted three score years and ten, and one Caleb Farley died in Hollis, April 5th, 1833, at the age of 102 years, 5 months. Many Hollis people are unable to give his pedigree, consequently we give it here.

1 George.

2 Caleb.

Caleb 2, had 1st, by his first wife Rebecca Hill, two children, the first being Caleb 3.

Caleb Jun., son of Caleb 2, b. 1667, June 28; m. 1686, April 8, Sarah Godfry of Haverhill. She d. 1704, Nov. 13; he m. 1707, Sept. 25, Lydia Haws. Ch. George, b. 1686-7, Jan. 26. Caleb, b. 1688, Jan. 6. John, b. 1690, May 22. Sarah, b. 1692, July 27. Mary, b 1694, Sept. 26. James, b. 1697, Sept. 8. Deborah, b 1698-9, Feb. 26. Jonathan, b. 1701, Oct. 2. Samuel, b. 1703, April.

James, son of Caleb 3, b. 1697, Sept. 8; m, 1728, May 17, Sarah Durrent, dau. of Thomas 3. He was dismissed to Hollis, in 1769. Ch. Thomas, b 1729, March 27. Caleb, b. 1730, Oct. 19. Sarah, b. 1733, April 16. Lyda, b. 1737-8, Jan. 13; m. John Conray. Mary, b. 1741, Dec. 18.

Caleb, son of James 4, b. 1730, Oct. 19; m. 1754, Oct. 17, Elizabeth Farley, dau. of Joseph 3. Capt. Farley removed to Hollis in 1765, and d. there 1833, April 5 aged 102 years. Ch. Elizabeth, b. 1755 Aug. 24. Joseph, b. 1757, May 1. Caleb, b. 1759, April 3. James, b. 1761, April 12. Benjamin, b. 1763 June 27. John, b. 1765, May 24. Thomas, b. 1769, Dec. 28. Abel, b. 17 July, 1773.

PEDIGREE OF CALEB'S WIFE ELIZABETH.

1 George.

2 Caleb.

By Caleb's second wife Lydia More, there were born eight children. The 6th was Joseph (3), b. 6 April, 1683; d. 19 Dec., 1752; m. Abigail Cook of Cambridge, 8 May, 1712. She died 18 Jan., 1753, aged 64 years.

They had issue:

i. Sary 4, b. Feb. 26th, 1713; d. in Oct., 1716.

ii. Joseph. b. Aug. 25th, 1714; d. Nov. 24th, 1762.

iii. Abigail, b. Dec. 18th, 1716.

iv. Lydia, b. April 30th, 1719; m. James Twist, June 27th, 1754.

v. Sarah, b. Aug. 1st, 1721; m. Josiah Blood, July 23d, 1741.

vi. Mary, b. Oct. 16th, 1723.

vii. Elizabeth, b Feb. 18th, 1725; m. Caleb Farley, Oct. 17, 1754.

viii. Caleb, b. Feb. 20th, 1728; d. June 2d, 1753.

ix. Ebenezer, b. May 15th, 1731; m. Hephzibah Wyman.

ANCESTRY OF JOANNA (PAGE) FARLEY.

(See page 20.)

PAGE or PAIGE Nathaniel 1, was in Roxbury in 1686. He is thought to have been the brother of Nicholas of Boston, 1665, who came from Plymouth, Eng. Gov. Joseph Dudley appointed Nathaniel 1 sheriff of Suffolk County. He bought and of George Grimes, and settled in Billerica (now Bedford) in 1688. He m

Joanna and d. "12-02-92" (Apr. 12 1692).
Ch. Nathaniel 2 b. about 1679. Elizabeth
m. John Simpkins of Boston. Sarah m.
Samuel Hill. James 2 d. young. Christopher b. 1690-1.

Nathaniel 2, son of Nathaniel 1, b. in
England, and came to New England
when about 14 years old. He m. Nov. 6,
1701, Susannah Lane, who d. 1746; m.
2d, 1748, Mary Grimes. He d. 1755. Ch.
Nathaniel 3, b. Sept. 4, 1702. John 3, b.
Oct. 11, 1704. Christopher 3, b July 16,
1707. Susannah, b. April 29, 1711. m.
Samuel Bridge of Lexington, d. 1735.
Joanna,,b. 1714, m. Josiah Fassett.

Christopher 2, son of Nathaniel 1, m
Joannah ——, who d. Oct. 27, 1719; m.
2d, May 23, 1720, Elizabeth, dau. of
Dea. George Reed of Woburn. He d. in
Hardwick, Mar. 10, 1774; she d. 1786,

Ch. Joanna, b. Aug. 10. 1717, m. Benj
Farley. Christopher 3, b. June 11, 1721.
m. Rebecca Haskell. William 3 b. May
2, 1723, m. Mercy Aiken. He d. Feb. 14
1790; she d. Feb. 19, 1823, aged 102
years. George 3, b. June 17, 1725, m.
Rosilla Whitcomb, d. 1781. Timothy 3,
b. May 24, 1727, m. Mary Foster of
Rochester. He d. Aug. 26, 1791; she d-
July 21, 1825, aged 93 years. His son
Timothy was the father of Rev. L. R.
Page, the historian of Cambridge. Jonas
3, b. Sept. 19, 1729. Elizabeth, b. Oct.
3, 1731. Lucy, b. Feb. 22, 1733-4, m.
Seth Lincoln of Newton. There were
born in Hardwick, Nathaniel 3, b. May
12, 1736, d. Jan. 6, 1816. John 3, b. July
6, 1738, d. April 14, 1811. Elizabeth, b,
June 11, 1743, m. Solomon Green of Lei.
cester.

FARLEY CHAPEL AND CASTLE.

FARLEY CASTLE.

The remains of Farley Castle, once so distinguished as the residence of Sir Thomas Hungerford and his proud line of successors, are now recognized only by a few embattled turrets, and by monumental effigies and inscriptions.

A curious fragment of painted glass in a window of the parish church (not the apse within the castle walls), commemorates the purchase of this Manor of Farley in the portrait of Sir Thomas Hungerford. This relic confirms what is related by Dugdale,—that Sir Thomas was buried in the north aisle of the church of St. Amee at Farley. Richard Colb Hoare, Bart.. says that the portrait of Sir Thomas is an accurate tracing from the glass window in the parish church.

The following account of Farley Castle, taken from an old survey, will prove interesting as throwing light on its ancient state, and the etching indicates the relative situations of the chapel and the principal entrance into the area of the castle.

"The sayde castell standeth in a Parke lenying unto a hill syde portly and very strongly buylded. having inward and outward wards. and in the inward ward many fayre chambers. a fayre large hall. on the hedde of which hall iij or iiij goodly greate chambers with fayre and strong rofs and dyvs other fayre lodgings with all man howsses of office. The Parke wherin the sayd castell standeth ys ij myles and iij q'rtes in circuite, a very fayre and p'kely grounde, beying envyroned rounde aboute with highe hylls. and in the myddes a broke, and depe rounyng Streme, rounynd throw it, and harde by the castell walls very well set with grete Okes and other woodde, whyche is valued to be worthe cccc li and is replenished weth xxxj dere of auntlet and xiiiij of roscall, and the Kings highness doeth gyce by reason of the sayd castell iii advowsons and ij chaunteyes, which ij chaunteyes doe stand w'ten the walls of the castell, and the sayd castell ys worthe in rentes. fermes and casualities————————."

Though the remains of this celebrated castle and mansion, etc., are very trifling, yet from the singularity of the sepulchral vault they merit the attention of every lover of antiquity. The lands are situated partly in Wilts and partly in Somerset. and lie between the town of Frome and city of Bath, and a Roman villa (lately discovered within the former demesnes), is now under investigation.

At Down Ampney, which is situated partly in Gloucestershire and partly in Wiltshire, we find the most perfect remains of a stately gateway leading to the mansion in which are some traces of the ancient building. This portal is flanked by two handsome turrets and is grand and appropriate in its style of architecture. This ancient mansion still retains more of its baronial grandeur than any existing residence of the Hungerfords, especially in its old hall and the before mentioned gateway.

The parish church also contained some

sepulchral monuments of its ancient pos-
sessors. We are informed by the historian
of Gloucestershire, Sir Robert Atkyns.
that Sir Thomas Hungerford purchased
the charter of a Free Warren at Down
Amprey 21, Richard II, A. D. 1398. He
was succeeded by his son Walter, who
died 27, Henry VI, A. D.. 1449, leaving
two sons, Robert, his heir, and Edmond,
on whom he settled the Down Ampney
estate, which continued in the family of
Hungerford until, from failure of male
issue, it devolved to Edmond Dunch, who
married the heiress of Hungerford. The
residence of the Dunchess was at Willen-
hom Co. of Berks.

"Farley Castle, Mar. 20, 1794, Somersetshire, Eng : Manor of Roger de Curcelle,
to whom it was granted by the Conqueror descended through the families of

Montfort, Burgath and Hungerford to Jo_
seph Houlton. its present owner."

From Gentleman's Magazine.

"The Hungerford family are all buried
in the chapel of this castle. In a window
on the north side of the chancel are two
large shields, one of them containing the
arms of the Hungerford family, with an
impalement which is entirely defaced."

From "History and Antiquities of Somersetshire," by Wm. Collinsman.

"Hungerfords of Willow, County of Somerset: By an inscription on the monu-
ment of Sir Thomas Hungerford of
Farley, bearing the date of 1398, we find
that the family was at that early period
possessed of the manor of Willow. The
parish register at this place does not go
back further than the year 1638. Giles
Hungerford, d. 1638; Jane Hungerford

wife of Giles. d. Oct. 11. 1679; John 3d son of Giles. d. 18 Jan., 1655; Ursula. 2nd daughter of Giles, d 18 July 1645; Giles, 2nd son ot Giles, d. Oct. 6, 1668, aged 33; Susanna, daughter of Giles, d. Sept., 1652; Edmond, son."

Hungerfords of Windrush, County of Oxford: "This branch of the Hungerford family appear to have been originally derived from Edward. second son of John of Down Ampney by Margaret Blount. He married Margaret, daughter of Sir John St John, and departed this life 1531. Inscription on a flat stone in the church is as follows :—

"Here lieth George Hungerford and by him Katharine his wife, daughter of Edward Fabian of Compton County of Burkesheere, Eng., by whom he had nine children: Edward, Anthony, Thom-

as, John. Jane, A'ne, Martha, 8th unin-
telligible, Eleanor, was interred June 16,
1597."

Jane Hungerford at Farley Castle
married Fabyan Farley of Bristol.

SIR THOMAS HUNGERFORD.

(The first known speaker of Parliament.)